W9-CQS-563

THE MAGIC SHOW MYSTERY

Created by **Gertrude Chandler Warner**

Illustrated by **Daniel Mark Duffy**

ALBERT WHITMAN & Company
Morton Grove, Illinois

You will also want to read:
Meet the Boxcar Children
A Present for Grandfather
Benny's New Friend
Benny Goes Into Business
Watch Runs Away
The Secret Under the Tree
Benny's Saturday Surprise

Library of Congress Cataloging-in-Publication Data

Warner, Gertrude Chandler, 1890-1979
The magic show mystery / created by Gertrude Chandler Warner;
illustrated by Daniel Mark Duffy.
p.   cm. —(The adventures of Benny and Watch)
Summary: After seeing a magician perform, Benny enlists his dog Watch to
help him put on his own magic show, but then both Watch and
Benny's magic bag disappear.
ISBN 0-8075-4939-8
[1. Magic tricks—Fiction. 2. Dogs—Fiction.] I. Duffy, Daniel M., ill. II. Title.
PZ7.W244Mag   1998
[E]--dc21   98-30605
CIP
AC

Copyright © 1998 by Albert Whitman & Company.
Published in 1998 by Albert Whitman & Company,
6340 Oakton Street, Morton Grove, Illinois 60053.
Published simultaneously in Canada by
General Publishing, Limited, Toronto.

10 9 8 7 6 5 4 3 2

The Boxcar Children

Henry, Jessie, Violet, and Benny Alden are orphans. They are supposed to live with their grandfather, but they have heard that he is mean. So the children run away and live in an old red boxcar. They find a dog, and Benny names him Watch.

When Grandfather finds them, the children see that he is not mean at all. They happily go to live with him. And, as a surprise, Grandfather brings the boxcar along!

Benny was at a birthday party.

A magician was doing tricks. He pulled a handkerchief from a hat and said, "Behold!"

A rabbit popped out of the hat!

"How did that rabbit get in there?" Benny Alden asked.

The man smiled. "A magician never tells his secrets."

The magician gave each guest a little book about magic tricks.

The party was over.

But Benny's fun with magic was just beginning.

"Come on, Watch," Benny said when he got home. "I need a helper. You get a cracker every time we do a magic trick."

Now, Watch didn't know much about magic. But he did know a lot about crackers.

At first Benny and Watch made a lot of mistakes. Benny clapped three times for Watch to carry in a bag of magic tricks. But Watch brought in an old boot instead.

Next, Benny clapped for Watch to pull a handkerchief from his old pink cup. Instead, Watch barked at a cat walking by.

After a lot of practice—and a lot of
crackers—Benny and Watch were ready.
"Henry, Jessie, Violet! Come see what
Watch and I can do!"

Benny clapped three times. In trotted Watch with the magic bag.

Out came a magic wand and a handkerchief.

Out came a box of animal crackers.

Out came the old cracked pink cup Benny had found when he lived in the boxcar with Henry, Jessie, and Violet.

"Behold my pink cup. Do you see it is empty?" Benny asked.

"I see that it is empty," said Henry.

"Behold! Do you see me covering this cup?"

"I see you covering it," said Jessie.

"Do you see my dog?" Benny asked.

Everyone looked at Watch.

Benny clapped again.

Swish! Watch pulled away the handkerchief.

"Behold! Crackers!"

"How did the crackers get in there?" Violet asked.

Benny just smiled. "A magician never tells his secrets."

Everyone clapped. Watch stood up on his hind legs until Benny fed him an animal cracker.

The next day Benny and Watch practiced magic tricks all over the neighborhood.

"I'm getting ready for a magic show," he told his friend Michael. "Want to see one of my tricks?"

Benny made a small ball appear in his empty pink cup.

"How did the ball get in there?" Michael asked.

Benny fed Watch a cracker. "A magician never tells his secrets."

At Beth's house, Benny poured clear water into his cup. He covered it with the handkerchief.

"Behold! I will make this water blue," Benny said. He clapped for Watch. *Swish!* Watch pulled away the handkerchief.

"It's blue!" Beth cried.

Watch stood up on his hind legs and waited for crackers.

But this time Benny forgot Watch's treat. He went off to play catch with Beth instead. No more crackers for Watch today!

Benny had one last trick up his
sleeve. He invited Violet to the boxcar.
"Turn around while I get ready."

Violet waited and waited. "What's
taking so long?"

"You can turn around now."

Benny clapped three times.

Nothing happened.

"Is this part of your new magic trick?" Violet asked.

Benny looked around. "Uh-oh. Where's Watch? Where's my magic bag? And my pink cup? They've disappeared, and I can't do my magic show without them!" Benny said.

Benny searched the house. "Watch!" he yelled.

"What's going on?" Mrs. McGregor asked. "Did you make Watch disappear? That would be an amazing trick!"

"It's not a trick. It's for real. Watch is gone, and so is my pink cup."

Then Benny looked up. "Hey, is that it?"

Mrs. McGregor looked up. "Sorry, Benny. That's Violet's thermos," she said. "I haven't seen your pink cup anywhere."

Benny opened the back door. "I'm going to search the whole neighborhood."

"Yoo-hoo!" Michael's grandmother called when she saw Benny. "Did you come by to show Michael more tricks?"

"I came by to *find* my magic tricks," Benny said.

What was that in Mrs. Teasdale's hand?

Benny took a closer look.
"Isn't this cup pretty?" Mrs. Teasdale asked. "It used to be my grandmother's."
"Oh," said Benny. "I thought it might be the pink cup I use for my tricks."

Next, Benny went over to Beth's house. Beth was playing in her room. What was that sticking out of Beth's toy box?

"My cup!" Benny cried.

Benny pulled away a ball and a catcher's mitt.

"Aw," he said. "It's a cup from a doll set."

Benny headed home. What was he going to do? His magic show was the next day.

He went into his backyard. With each step, he heard a sound. *Crunch. Crunch. Crunch.*

First, Benny found a
tiger cracker under the
maple tree.

Then he spotted
two zebra crackers a
few steps later.

A path of animal crackers zig-zagged
all the way to . . .

. . . Watch's doghouse!

Benny saw Watch. Watch saw Benny.
Watch stopped licking his lips.

"What did you eat, Watch?" Benny asked.
Watch looked away.

"Come on," Benny said. "Did you take the animal crackers and my pink cup, too?"

Watch's tail drooped. He crawled into his dog house.

Benny peeked inside. "Behold! My old pink cup!"

"So you were the one who made my cup disappear!" Benny cried. "From now on, let *me* do the magic tricks, Watch!"

The next day everyone came to
Benny's magic show.

Benny held his cup upside down. It was empty. He covered the cup. Benny clapped. *Swish!* Watch pulled away the handkerchief.

"Behold!" Benny said. "Crackers!"

"How did the crackers get in there?" Grandfather asked.

Benny just smiled. "A magician never tells his secrets. But Watch *always* gets his crackers."

Do you want to know Benny's magic secrets? He hid the crackers and ball up his sleeve. As he covered the cup with the handkerchief, he let the crackers and ball slip into the cup.

To turn clear water into colored water, put a tiny drop of food dye in the bottom of the cup. Quickly show everyone the empty cup before you cover it with the handkerchief or scarf. (Don't worry, they won't see a speck of food dye.) Then just pour clear water into the cup. Ta-da! The water is blue!